I WANT TO PAINT
MY BATHROOM BLUE

I WANT TO PAINT
MY BATHROOM BLUE

BY RUTH KRAUSS

PICTURES BY MAURICE SENDAK

HARPER COLLINS PUBLISHERS

I want to paint my bathroom blue
—my papa won't let me paint it blue—
once I painted a rocking-chair blue
and it was pretty.
I want to paint my kitchen yellow

and my sitting room white with turtles
and all my ceilings green.

and here

And I'd put a window here

and here

and here

and here

and on the outside walls of my house should
be a big big picture—a funny big picture like
the mother is blushing because her two
children put their feet in the cake—

and I'll sprinkle seeds all over the land.

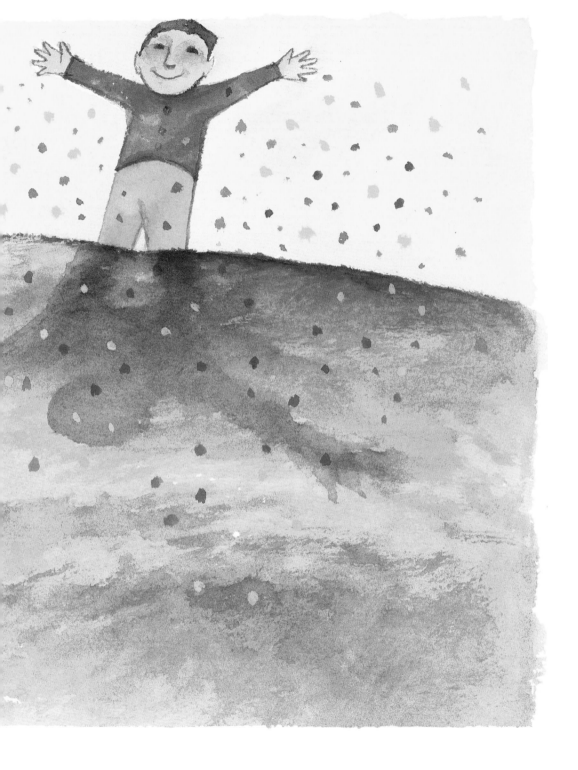

I'll make a big white door
with a little pink doorknob—
and a song about the doorknob goes
a doorknob a doorknob
a dear little doorknob
a dearknob a dearknob
a door little dearknob—

and stairs going up to another floor
and upstairs a horse in the bedroom.

I'll make a house the kind I dream about
not the kind I see. It's a house like a rainbow.
And my friends all live with me there.

And someday will be grass and trees—

and I'd make an ocean.